THE ADVENTURES OF

Mischief Mishka

in Central Park

Written & Edited by Amber Satterfield

Illustrated by Pet Creations

Book 1 of The Adventures of Mischief Mishka Series

For information and permissions, contact the author at contact@theadventuresofmischiefmishka.com or visit www.theadventuresofmischiefmishka.com

ISBN: 979-8-9851779-0-9

THE ADVENTURES OF Mischief Mishka

In Central Park

Once upon a day from far, far, away, came a ball of fur named Mishka in search of her next adventure. Moving from the city of mountains to the city of skyscrapers, Mishka and her family found themselves right in the center of New York City!

They were filled with excitement and glee at what was upon them and the adventures they were going to have!

With pure excitement, Mishka had run outside to stand on her New York City stoop and looked around in awe of all that surrounded her.

The tall buildings. The bright lights. All the noise and the cars. And so many people!

"Look at all of these new friends and the mischievious adventures that I can have here!" she said with complete joy.

To Mishka's delight, two new friends had come over to say, "Henlo there fwend! Are you new here?"

Mishka shook her head eagerly, excited to make her first friends in this new city.

"Then you must go to Central Park! It's filled with lots of adventures and so many places to explore!", said Frankie, the Husky.

Mishka leaned in to listen intently as her new friends told her all about their adventures in this perfectly sounding place. She imagined all the mischief she could get in to!

Mishka decided right then that she must go!

So, off Mishka and her mom went to explore Central Park!

As they first entered, Mishka couldn't stop looking at the beauty all around her. She had never seen a park so big before!

And then, atop of a hill, she spotted something! A huge castle right in the middle of the park! She hurriedly ran up the steps to find herself at the Belvedere Castle.

The castle was so magical and made her feel like a pretty Princess. She just needed her tiara to make it perfect!

Mishka and her mom sat at the castle and took in the view of the park.

Then she noticed something down the hill. She squinted her eyes to try to see what the creature was that caught her eye. She had never seen anything like it before. She sprinted full speed in excitement to see what it could be! It was a cute little animal with a small head that popped right out from underneath a shell. As Mishka had come closer, its head disappeared!

"Boop!" Mishka said, as she patted the top of its shell with her paw. "Henlo fwend, what are you?"

"Hi, I'm a turtle. My name is Zippy.", it said, as it shyly began to pop its head out from the shell.

"I've never met a turtle before. It's so nice to meet you, Zippy!", said Mishka.

"It's nice to meet you too", Zippy said with a friendly smile forming on its face.

BOOP!

At that moment, Mishka had begun to hear a cute little squeaking noise coming from a nearby tree. Excited to find out what it was, she had run over to explore closer. She jumped excitedly and ran around the tree looking for what could be making that noise.

Then this cute little critter runs down the tree to meet her. "Hey there, dog, I am Oakley the squirrel. Do you want to play?", asked the squirrel.

"Boy do I!", Mishka exclaimed excited to make another friend.

Mishka barked and ran and jumped around the tree as Oakley scurried up and down the trunk just out of her reach. Both laughed and enjoyed this moment while making a new friend.

Thirsty from all the running and barking, Mishka found a small pond where she could get a drink. As she was lapping up the water, she looked up and saw these beautiful animals floating on the water like magic.

They flapped their wings and splashed around in the water.

Mishka stared in confusion and curiosity.

"How are they just floating on the water?" she thought to herself.

Every time she gets in the water she sinks straight down and has to swim just to keep her head up.

Quack!
Quack!

Mishka followed them as they magically floated away.

She ran up to the top of Bow Bridge and called down to them "Henlo fwend. What are you?"

The ducks looked up at her with amusement. "Quack! Quack! Quack! We are ducks" they answered. "This is how we swim" and they flipped over in the water and showed off their cute little webbed feet to Mishka.

In awe, Mishka just watched them as they bathed and swam in the water.

All of a sudden, she heard a noise off in the distance. The curiosity got the better of her and she was off to find out what it was.

She stumbled upon a long walkway called The Mall.

She was immediately surrounded by lots of people, food carts, and shopping huts along the path. Then she sees it. A hotdog stand. Her tummy began to rumble with hunger.

"Boy, I am hungry now. Don't they say that New York City has the best hot dogs?" she asked her Mom, "Let's find out!" They grabbed a couple hot dogs for lunch and made their way down The Mall.

"Yummm, they do have the best hot dogs!" Mishka says as she licks her whiskers.

While they enjoyed their lunch, off in the distance they heard a magical symphony of the most beautiful music they'd ever heard. Mishka strolled down a large set of stairs, curious as to what she might find. She happened upon the echo of a voice that sounded like an angel cascading off the walls and ceiling of the Bethesda Terrace.

Beyond the voice, she noticed the Bethesda Fountain and it was filled with water! "No better time to enjoy music while frolicking around in the water" she thought as she mischievously pranced over to the fountain and jumped straight into the water with a big splash. After she played and laughed for awhile, she hopped out and gave herself a good shake.

"This may be my favorite place in the whole wide world!", she said to her mom.

As they left the fountain, they ran into the sweetest little girl they'd ever met named Maizie!

"Oh my goodness, She is so furry!", exclaimed Maizie, as she ran over to hug Mishka and all of her fluff. Mishka had immediately fallen in love with her. "Do you want to go and find some acorns for the squirrels?" asked Maizie.

"Boy do I!" Mishka thought as she jumped with excitement and ran up to walk with Maizie.

After finding a bunch of acorns and attempting to feed them to squirrels, Maizie sadly had to leave. "We will have another play date soon, I promise", she said as she kissed Mishka's little nose and said goodbye.

As she watched Maizie leave, Mishka saw something else she'd never seen before. A bunch of dogs that look exactly like her!

Overjoyed, she ran full speed towards the other group of Samoyeds.

"Mom, hurry up!", she yelled behind her as she met up with the others.

They all ran around, jumping and barking "Henlo! Henlo! Henlo fwend!" they all said to each other.

They spent hours making lots of friends and getting lots of cuddles in the afternoon sun.

But then the sky had begun to get darker...

Thunder had blasted out in the sky, "BOOM!"

As the rain started to come down, Mishka and her mom quickly headed for home. That's when Mishka spotted some other dogs playing and splashing in the puddles. Before Mishka's mom could stop her, Mishka ran off into the rain to meet them!

Mishka grabbed a stick and ran as fast as she could as her new friends chased after her in the wet grass and mud.

"Come and get me!" she barked, as she laughed and splashed around. The other dogs were laughing and running at her heels to try to grab the stick.

One thing Mishka didn't realize though...

By getting this muddy and dirty, it meant that she would need a bath when she got home!

"Oh no!", she thought. "I hate getting baths!"

She pouted and gave her very best little puppy dog eyes to her mom but to no avail; bath time was definitely needed.

They had made their way home together in the rain and mud enjoying the evening together strolling through the park.

Central Park had become even more magical in the rain, they realized, as the people cleared out and the noise stopped.

After her bath, Mishka slipped into her pajamas and climbed onto her favorite sleeping spot on the couch.

"What a wonderful day of adventures", she thought as she lay her head down for the night.

A smile filled her face as she thought about all of the new friends she made in this new City she now calls home.

"This is my favorite place in the whole, wide world and I can't wait for every day to be like today."

And with that, she closed her eyes and fell fast asleep.

(Not) The End

More Adventures to be continued....

Dedications:

This book is Dedicated to my parents who were
my biggest supporters of all the big ideas in
my head and my crazy life adventures.

Acknowledgments:

I would like to thank Pet Creations for being open to the idea of
doing book illustrations for the first time! You guys have been a
dream to work with and I look forward to our future projects together!
Thank you to Mishka's favorite friend, Elliot, whom she would literally go crazy over!
Also, a big thanks to my mom for being my support throughout this
whole project as well as my other books I am soon to publish!

Other Books by this Author:

The Adventures of Mischief Mishka in The Big Apple (Coming Soon!)
Thriving with Autoimmune Diseases (a memoir - Coming Soon!)

Lightning Source UK Ltd.
Milton Keynes UK
UKRC032203221121
394387UK00001B/10
9798985177909